MARY ELIZA

Mary Parker Donaldson

To Barbara & Truman Toy
Love & Hugs
Mary Parker Donaldson

ISBN 978-1-61225-070-0

Copyright © 2011 Mary Parker Donaldson
All Rights Reserved

No part of this publication may be reproduced in any form or stored, transmitted or recorded by any means without the written permission of the author.

Published by Mirror Publishing
Milwaukee, WI 53214
www.pagesofwonder.com

Printed in the USA

For my wonderful husband, Wilber, who brought much love and wisdom into my life; for my parents, Catherine and Vernon Parker, for life's lessons shared, and for my grandmother Mary Eliza who was my inspiration in more ways than I could ever imagine. Special thanks to my son, Tony and wife, Ginny for believing in me. For all those dear friends who have shared in this endeavor, thank you for your love and patience.

BACKGROUND

Mary Eliza Flynn was my Grandmother but not by birth. She adopted my Mother. Little did I realize what a profound effect she would have on my life. Ahead of her time, she was. God bless her. This is her story, as best I know it. I don't believe you'll easily forget her. If you are fortunate, she will remind you of someone special you have met along the way. At least, I believe you will enjoy knowing this hard working, spirited lady I so fondly knew as Ganna. Her pet name for me was Dump, short for Dumpling.

CHAPTER 1

The train was almost empty that day. Mary could see her Papa standing at the station door, pipe gripped in his teeth, head down, not able to look her way. She was the first one to leave home. Martinsburg, West Virginia was a railroad town and Papa had worked on trains since he'd come from Ireland some forty years ago. He could have expected to see at least one of his eight living children leave this way.

Mary was seventeen by five months to the day. The day was May 7, 1908. Her bright bronze hair curled about the edges of the beige knit cloche Mammy made for her birthday. The purse, made to match, contained a one-way ticket to Washington, D. C., ten dollars, fifty-two cents and written directions to a hotel in the city. Mary had been saving every penny she could spare since as far back as she could remember. She was leaving for what she hoped would be a far better life than the one she had known or could expect in the remote mill and farm town of Martinsburg, West Virginia.

She gazed at the countryside all dressed in Spring colors. Her thoughts were of the family she was leaving behind. The years there had been hard ones. Her heart raced. She was alone and felt every chilling moment of it.

The train loped along out of sight of everything she had ever known. Mary was becoming caught up in the beauty of the passing scenery and could only wonder about a man she barely knew and the offer he made not a month ago. She felt a twinge of desperation but it soon passed as her thoughts were interrupted by the call of the Conductor.

"Tickets, collecting tickets" he muttered. He smiled as she nervously handed him her ticket. Her thoughts turned again back to her Mammy and the day she told her of her plan. Mammy smiled and said, "Take a chance Mary, you've never lacked courage and I know you will be all right. Work hard and mind your manners and don't forget your Mammy and those who love you." Mammy was a plain looking woman, small in stature but always seemed beautiful to Mary. Her Mother was strong in will and forthright with her children. Mammy was a constant source of strength when the children called upon her for any kind of support. She was the only one Mary had witnessed who could reason with Papa and had her way most of the time. Papa was hard-headed, silent, and stubborn. His only joy was his visits to The Loyal Order of the Elks where he'd lift a beer or more with his pals. Papa loved beer. He kept his money in his sock and was known to be a tightwad at the club. He told good stories though and some of the men would buy him a brew just to listen to his yarns.

Mary thought about her brothers, Dave and Charlie. They loved the train and where it would take them. Maybe they'd follow her sometime soon. As young children, the three of them would often play around the train yards, hopping freights to places like Hagerstown, Maryland and then catching the train back home. They met some pretty strange folks that way. One time Dave and Charlie went off in a boxcar without Mary. They were gone three days, not leaving the boxcar and with nothing to eat or drink. They slept with their shoes on. Their feet were so swollen they could not stand for long. When a worker found them, the boys were so scared they confessed immediately their Papa worked for the railroad and he was contacted. They were sent back home on the next train.

At home, Mammy cried as Charlie, Sr. took the belt to them. That was their last train adventure and it was a while until they were able to sit down with any comfort.

The Flynn's were a close family, mostly out of necessity. Their home in town was a two story, shotgun arrangement. The living room, dining room, and kitchen were separated by open arches and a hallway ran from front to back door. There was a stairway just to the left of the front door leading up to three bedrooms. Mammy and Papa's room was at the top of the stairs. There was a room for the girls, Florence, Mary, Sue, and Lucy and a room for the boys, Bud, Charlie, Dave, and Tom. In birth order there was Bud, Florence, Mary, Charlie, Sue, Dave, Lucy, and Tom. There had been a ninth child, a boy. The poor sick baby died after being given a fatal dose of prescribed medicine. The pharmacist had made the error. In those days, nothing much was done in cases like that and the family had little recourse but to let the law handle it. Mary and the others never knew the outcome.

There wasn't much of a backyard. There was room for a privy, small garden, a well house, a chicken coop, and a pig pen. Just near the back door were two posts with a line stretched to the privy and back to the posts for hanging out the wash. There was no need for a place to play as there was never time for that. There was an earthen cellar used for storing canned goods, root vegetables, hanging hams, a wash tub, a coal furnace and what few tools Papa used. There was also a large wood pile covered in part by a piece of tin. The wood was used for a cook stove.

Like most of the others, Mary had received three years of schooling and then worked in the Sock Mill with her older brother, Bud and older sister, Florence. All of the children followed suit. The youngest boy, Tom, finished the fifth grade, a reward for being such a good student, and then followed the others to the mill. The children were paid fifteen cents per week for their labor and Papa allowed them to keep a penny for themselves.

That penny could buy a piece of candy. Two cents could buy an ice cream cone to share. Their pay was delivered to Papa by each child every Friday. On weekends in the summer, the children would also work on a farm near town for pennies a day.

CHAPTER 2

Mary could not believe how fast her life was changing. It was dreamlike. She pulled the note from her purse. It read, Mr. Callahan, Colonial Hotel, E Street at North Capital Streets, N. W., Washington, D. C. Mr. Callahan was a customer at the City Café in Martinsburg just about a month ago. Mary was his waitress and not recognizing him, had asked him if he was a stranger in town. He explained he was there to bury his only brother and was on his way back to Washington, D. C. on the morning train. He was a distinguished looking man in his early fifties and neatly dressed in a stylish gray wool suit.

He ordered breakfast and watched Mary as she served three other customers nearby. She was as cordial and as efficient as the most skilled waitresses he'd observed in his many years in the restaurant business. She busied herself clearing tables, slicing pies and making certain his coffee cup remained full.

"What's your name, girl?" he asked.

"Mary Eliza Flynn," Mary replied. "Why do you ask anyway?" Mary added.

"Mary, I am manager of the restaurant in the Colonial Hotel in Washington, D. C. and if you have reason to come there, I'll have a job for you as a waitress, young lady."

Mary said, "Please write that down for me, sir, and I just might take you up on that."

Mr. Callahan left Mary the biggest tip she'd ever received.

She thought about what Mr. Callahan had said and couldn't shake the feeling that she should go for it. As the next few days went by she could think of nothing else but a chance to be on her own and make a good life. She thought about Mr. Callahan and how he looked so professional in his nifty suit and dark blue tie. She judged him to be a gentleman of the finest quality. When she saw her sister, Sue, she told her what she was bound to do.

"I'm packing my things and heading straight to Washington and if all goes like I hope, I'll send for you and Charlie and whoever else wants to leave here." Sue's reaction was instant. She hugged Mary and the girls danced with joy. Sue was the prettiest of all the girls. Her long hair was a soft reddish blonde and hung in natural waves over her shoulders. Her eyes were a lively, clear blue, and she was almost six inches taller than Mary at five foot, six inches. Years of hard work and eating lightly had contributed to her beautiful figure. She was as sweet as she was pretty and Mammy worried about Sue and how popular she was with the boys. She had no need to worry though as Sue was too busy working and helping at home to find trouble.

The girls talked for hours and Sue helped Mary with her packing as they chatted about what the future might hold for both of them. The thought of a glorious future in a far away place sent the girls thinking of things they'd never thought before like where they might live and what famous folks they might meet. Mary made Sue promise she wouldn't tell the family until Mary had a chance to do that in her own way and time. Sue's reward would be the first of the family Mary would send for as she got settled in her new home. That was reward enough for Sue.

Mary worked another week and socked away all the tip money for the week at the café. She gave her notice on Saturday and explained to Miss Lizzie she would be going out of town to work. That evening at supper, she asked to have a word with Papa and Mammy as soon as the kitchen was clean. She sat at the kitchen table with droplets of sweat beading on her brow. This was unexpected territory and even though Mary was seventeen, she didn't know what her parent's reaction would be.

Choosing her words carefully, she said that a most proper gentleman, Mr. Callahan, Manager of the Colonial Hotel in

Washington, D. C. had offered her a job as a waitress if she were to be in the city, that he had been impressed with her skills at the Café and had come home to bury his brother. As luck would have it, Papa had also attended the funeral of his close friend, Patrick Callahan and had met his brother, Paul at the funeral. He had talked with him and judged him to be a decent man like his late brother. He'd even remembered him as a child. Papa was slow to respond and Mary feared the worst. Mammy's eyes welled with tears but said not a word. Mary was extra special to Mammy. Mary was not the prettiest of the girls, more of a tomboy, and more outspoken than the rest. She was a hand full and hard-headed at times but worked hard and always carried her load. She was also a fighter and Mammy knew Mary could handle most any situation and would do it with a good and honest heart.

Papa looked Mary in the eyes and finally said, we'll miss you Mary. Mary jumped out of her chair and hugged her parents and flew up the stairs to share her overwhelming exuberance with Sue and the others. Papa held Mammy's hand. Florence had recently announced her engagement to Martin and Bud had proposed to Minnie and they were looking for a home. Watching the children grow and leave home was natural but never easy.

As the train pulled in to Union Station, Mary showed her note from Mr. Callahan to the Conductor and he directed her to the information desk in the middle of the huge station.

The clerk directed Mary to go out the Station front door and look to her right. She would be able see the big red brick hotel just across the street from Union Station. Her future was there if Mr. Callahan was the gentlemen she thought he was. No time to doubt now; I've come this far. Life is too short to wake up with regrets, thought Mary. She made her way to the front desk of the hotel and asked for Mr. Callahan. The clerk asked a bellboy to tell Mr. Callahan he had a guest.

"Mary, what a delightful surprise!" offered Mr. Callahan. "You must be here to go to work." She smiled and declared she was ready to do just that. "Do you have a place to stay?"

"No," replied Mary.

"I know just the place around the corner; it's Mrs. O'Brien's Boarding House and I'll take you right around to meet her. She runs a clean place and serves good food so let's see if she has room for you, Mary. I'll be wanting you to start work at 5:30 in the morning," he said. Mary felt as if she were in a dream.

Sue and the girls wouldn't believe her luck though they always used to tease her about being the lucky one. It could have backfired. Mary was in for more surprises that day.

Mrs. O'Brien was a big bosomed, ox of a woman. Her red hair was streaked with gray and she gathered it in a knot high on the top of her head. Her eyes were light blue and danced a jig as she talked to Mary about the general rules of the boarding house.

"Mind you child, I'll have no guests beyond the parlor and your rent will be due on each Saturday morning by noon or out you'll go."

Mary quickly agreed and was shown a small room on the third floor facing the street.

Mrs. O'Brien explained, "Your dirty sheets and towels will be placed outside the kitchen in the bin on Saturday morning. Replacements will be put on your bed later that day. Breakfast is served between five and seven a.m., supper between five and seven p.m. and meals are included in the rent. If you miss them, you miss them. If you come in after ten p.m. take off your shoes and don't wake the other boarders. That's it Mary so do you want it or not?"

Mary quickly said, "To be sure I do, and pleased and that."

Mrs. O'Brien smiled. She had a good feeling about this one.

On the way back to the hotel, Mary grabbed Mr. Callahan's arm and stopped him in his tracks. "Mr. Callahan, before we start working together, I must confess I need your help." "What is it, Mary?" he asked. "Mr. Callahan, I can count but I cannot read or write so how can I write orders for the cook?"

He smiled, "how'd you post your orders at the City Café?" he asked. "I just remembered what the customers said and told Miss Lizzie."

"Mary, it's not a problem here as our menu is numbered and it will be easy for you to remember." "There are only three choices on the breakfast menu, 1. Eggs Benedict, 2. House Omelet, or 3. Bakery basket and mixed fruit of the day. Think you can remember that?" Mary blushed and grinned, wiped her freckled brow and declared she could do that. Mr. Callahan explained that the lunch and dinner meals were served buffet style and all Mary would do is serve the drinks and give the customer a check if she were asked to serve those meals. Good fortune was still with her.

Back at the Colonial Hotel, Mr. Callahan introduced Mary to Pierre, a genuine French chef from Bordeaux, France. She met Charles, the Maitre d', Marsha Fay Weed and Linda Lee Burgess, both seasoned waitresses. They would be working the day shift with Mary.

Mary joined the girls each morning at 5:30 a.m. to set tables and prepare coffee. They began serving breakfast at 6 a.m., stayed on through the lunch hour, and also prepared the tables for the dinner meal. The girls were more than willing to teach Mary every trick so that she could carry her load as there was no time for mistakes. Mary felt right at home except for one thing. The dining room was breathtaking. Mary had not witnessed such a beautiful room in all her life. It was more elegant than the finest home in Martinsburg where she once applied for a position as maid. The room was done in lovely green and gold trimmed wallpaper. The tables were covered with white over green linen and the chairs were Burgundy velvet and cherry wood. There were five large chandeliers overhead made of fine crystal and gold. It was magnificent!

Pierre was a good man but was subject to fits of artistic temper. Mary watched him cook every time there was an extra moment. She was enchanted with the beauty of the dishes he prepared and loved it when he'd call on her to taste his entrees. Of course, Pierre was flattered with the attention and was inspired by it much to the delight of Mr. Callahan. Marsha Faye and Linda Lee were lovely girls and fast friends to Mary. The girls had spent their entire lives in the city and enjoyed Mary's stories about growing up in West Virginia in a large family. She told them about the brothers and sisters swimming nude in the quarry so they wouldn't have to explain their wet clothes to Mammy when coming home from working on the Godwin's farm on summer weekends. She told then about riding the boxcars with her brothers and stealing her sister, Lucy's, ice cream cone, running to the backyard and locking the privy door to enjoy it on a hot July day. She told them about working in the sock mill, killing a chicken for dinner, and working at the café as the only waitress.

Marsha had a beautiful, creamy complexion and an infectious laugh, snorting between giggles. Linda Lee had huge brown eyes and short curly black hair. She was tiny and had exceptionally thin legs. Mary wondered how those legs could move those long, skinny feet so well. Linda Lee seemed to move as if the wind just carried her through the dining room. The girls all disliked Maude, the cashier. Maude was from New York City and continuously talked about how great it was in New York, how much smarter and more fashion conscious the people who lived there were compared to D. C., how much the rest of the world just didn't measure up, especially her coworkers. She made it her daily duty to inform Mr. Callahan of each event of the day according to Maude. Maude told Mr. Callahan about the guest in Room 208 who would kiss the hands of the waitresses and how Linda Lee would encourage him. Maude tattled on Mary for giving a crying child a big hug and a donut not listed on the check. She told a story about Marsha one time too many. Marsha had not charged one of the regular patrons for a scoop of ice cream on his slice of apple pie. To get even, Marsha placed a big wad of well-chewed Double Mint gum on Maude's chair. She was able to distract Maude as she took her seat at the desk. By the end of the shift, Maude was securely stuck to her chair and the girls all but rolled on the floor with laughter as Maude pulled her bodacious backside off her chair. Mr. Callahan was relieved when Maude gave her immediate notice.

CHAPTER 3

Mrs. O'Brien reminded Mary of her sweet Mammy in the way she went about preparing the meals. Mrs. O's day started at 3 a.m. She would set the table in the dining room for breakfast. Meals were served family style and empty dishes were replaced with more freshly prepared food. She opened the dining room to folks off the street if there were extra places at the table and charged twenty-five cents per meal. The rest of the day was devoted to cleaning, preparation of the next meal and other routine household chores.

Every day was laundry day since there was only so much room to hang the linens. Groceries were delivered three times per week and ice delivered daily. Mrs. O'Brien canned her own vegetables and fruit in season. Thank the Lord for Mr. Peavey, a long time border and local banker. He also kept the books for the Boarding House. Mrs. O. had known Mr. Peavey most of her life. He was a good friend and her oldest boarder. Mrs. O'Brien tried to keep a maid to help her but found they were either lazy, untrustworthy, or just ran off to an easier job.

When Mary had been there a few months, she caught Mrs. O'Brien hanging sheets one day. "Mrs. O'Brien, I'm about to change my hours at the hotel and wait the supper meal instead of the morning shift," Mary explained. "I'll be free each morning and until 3 p.m. each day. I am an early riser and I was wondering if you'd be wanting some help here"? Mrs. O'Brien could certainly use the help. She hadn't had anyone to last more than a few weeks since her late husband, Ben, died over a year ago.

"Mary, I'm hard to work for, I suppose" said Mrs. O'Brien. "I'm set in me ways of doing things and I expect me wishes to be followed to the letter." She went on, "We'll try it for a week or so and if you can keep up and master the job as I want it done, we'll go with it." Mary smiled, bent over and picked up a sheet to hang it on the line.

"Stop, Mary, we must fold them in half to make room for as many of them as we can set out, so just watch and I'll show you how to do it."

Mary pitched in and worked both jobs every day thereafter except Sundays. At the end of her workday, she'd lay out her clean uniform, take her bath and go right to bed. Sunday was her day of rest. After washing her uniforms and preparing for the next week, she'd ask Mr. Peavey to write a letter to Mammy at least one Sunday each month and talk with him about saving money. She'd go for long walks around the Capitol and downtown as far as the White House and back. Mary never lost the feeling that the city was the most beautiful place to live and work there ever could be and never tired of discovering as much as she could about it.

If only Mammy would see the city, she thought. She was sure her Papa had not seen it. His job on the railroad had always taken him west and north of Martinsburg. If he'd been here, he would have been telling stories about it as he did about all the other places he'd seen. He'd often talked about Kansas City and how big and fancy it was there.

Each Sunday Mary counted her money and gave most of it to Mr. Peavey to put in her account at the bank. She had many dreams and among them was to help her brothers and sisters move to D.C. and have a grand time and an opportunity to get out of the mills and farms of West Virginia.

Two years passed quickly. Mary's oldest sister, Florence had married Martin Price, a hard working mill worker from Hagerstown, Maryland. They had started a family and Florence was the mother of a baby girl and kept a nice home for them. Florence wrote Mary a letter from time to time keeping her informed about her own life and also about the family back in Martinsburg. Her oldest Brother, Bud, had married his childhood sweetheart, Minnie and lived a few blocks away from the old home place. He worked for the railroad and they had not started a family. Mary never felt she knew Bud very well. He was six years old when she was born. From time to time, Mary would ask Mr. Peavey to answer Florence's letters. Florence was five years older than Mary and the kindest and wisest lady she knew. She had always been a strong, silent and a graceful influence on all her siblings. She was never involved in childish squabbles and treated all the little ones with the greatest respect. She was a natural lady and much respected even by her parents. Mary missed her so much.

Mary had learned to cook most of the dishes prepared by Chef Pierre. She had done well helping Mrs. O'Brien and had learned what it took to clean and care for a boarding house including how much food to prepare for the patrons who joined the regulars on weekends. Mary often helped with the canning and preserving of food in season. She loved to make watermelon pickles and chow-chow relish. She'd help with canning tomatoes, green beans, and corn. Putting by fresh vegetables and foods in season was the secret to providing good food at the Boarding House all year round. She knew she had saved enough extra money to buy a one-way ticket for sister, Sue to come to D. C.

Right after the Christmas holidays, Sue packed her suitcase and joined Mary at the Boarding House. She got a job as a waitress at the Athens Grill on Pennsylvania Avenue and within six months had married William Millios, the son of the owner. The newlyweds had a small apartment near the restaurant and Sue continued to work until she gave birth to a beautiful red haired boy, William Millios, Jr., nicknamed Snooky by the family. Sue's husband provided well for them and Sue was able to quit work and enjoy her son and a new home they shared in Northeast Washington.

Brother Charlie was the next to find his home in Washington. Charlie was the closest brother in age to Mary. He was a hard worker and had a more easy going nature than Mary. Early in World War I Charlie was wounded and released from the Navy. He'd been a cook on a ship. After being discharged, he found a job as handyman at the Harrington Hotel on Pennsylvania Avenue. He had a room in the basement there so that he'd be available whenever he was needed. He also saved as much of his pay as possible. He eventually married and opened his own restaurant at Seventh and H Streets, downtown. His wife Lucille was a divorcee with a beautiful little girl named Shirley. Two years later Lucille gave birth to another daughter, Wendy. It was time for Charlie to buy a home for the family and take on a second job to give his family all the things Lucille had wanted them to enjoy. A good friend managed the restaurant and Charlie bought a cab. He drove the cab and checked on the restaurant each day and all was going well. It was good to have family close once again.

Sister Lucy eloped with Earl Small and they found their way to Washington too. Lucy was the smallest and youngest of the girls. She had dark curly hair, a dainty figure and big, brown eyes. She had always been sickly and had not worked since marrying Earl. Lucy was never able to have children and she truly wanted a family. She was sweet and sensitive and spent all her time decorating her small apartment and caring for her happy husband. Earl was a painter, a man of few words and a hard worker who adored his wife. Their apartment was near the boarding house and the couple visited with Mary occasionally on Sunday afternoons. Brother Tom joined the Navy and after the WWI, married a hometown girl, Elsie and the couple stayed in Martinsburg. Tom and Elsie bought a small grocery store with the help of Bud. They had one son, Tom, Jr. Tom Sr. was handsome. He was tall, blue-eyed, with curley brown hair like his Papa. In fact, he favored Papa as did Florence, Dave, and Lucy. The others had their Mammy's red hair. Mammy had always made it clear that she wasn't a Flynn, she was a Ward.

Brothers Dave and John had been to England in World War I. As soon as the war was over, they both headed for Washington. Dave became a fireman in nearby Virginia and John was a cook at the Gaiety Buffet on Ninth Street, N. W. next to the Gaiety House of Burlesque. He learned to cook in the Navy and was good at it and loved the atmosphere of the grill. Mary so enjoyed having so many brothers and sisters close again.

Mr. Callahan watched Mary blossom into a confident,

hard working, and competent young lady. She never truly learned to read and write but her love of numbers, adding and subtracting and counting money came naturally. Mr. Callahan wasn't surprised that day in May when Mary asked to speak with him privately after the dinning room closed.

"Mr. Callahan, I must tell you that you changed my life and I'll miss seeing you each day but I must leave you now."

Looking somewhat startled he said, "Mary, what are you saying?" Mary bowed her head and starred at her shoes. Moments passed and she lifted her head revealing a huge smile. With tears forming in her blue eyes, she said, "Mrs. O'Brien is selling the Boarding House………..TO ME!" she squealed. With that she began to cry and laugh and sat right down on the floor to do it.

"My God in heaven, that's outstanding girl!" said Mr. Callahan. "Sure and I'm that proud of you and I wish you the best o' luck!" He continued, "Mary, you have always amazed me with your hard work and positive attitude. Why, I don't think you've missed a day of work in the years you've been working here." He hesitated and said, "Is Mrs. O'Brien in good health; she's not ill is she?"

"Oh, no," said Mary. "She's had enough and wants to open a small restaurant in Georgetown near her brother's home and move in with him." Mr. Callahan sighed in relief. "I've been with you here at the hotel for seven years now, Mr. Callahan and I'm that grateful to you for taking me on and making sure I learned to do things well and proper." She continued, "You are such a fine gentleman and I hope you will come and visit me at Flynn's Boarding House."

Mr. Callahan took Mary's hand and helped her to her feet. He gave here a hug and assured her that she had not seen the last of him and wished her good fortune.

Mr. Peavey sat down after breakfast with Mary and they worked out a system for managing Flynn's Boarding House. Mary had a quick wit and an infectious laugh. Her laugh reminded Mr. Peavey of a chicken announcing the laying of a really big egg. Mary said, "Mr. Peavey, would you help me learn to write me name?" She continued to explain," I've watched some folks do it and it looks like it could be fun." She let out a cackle and a wink and picked up a pencil as if ready to write.

Mr. Peavey said, "I'll be happy to show you but I'll have to show you again if you should marry and change your name." That thought had not occurred to Mary although she certainly liked men and had been attracted to a few for their good looks and good manners. The truth of it, at twenty-four, she'd never been asked on a date. She was certainly pretty enough. Her hair was a shiny mass of honey-red waves. Her blue eyes were full of mischief and her skin tanned and slightly freckled. At five foot tall, she was slim at the waist and big at the breast. Her problem was simple. If she wasn't working or preparing for work, she was asleep. Her friends and family visited while she worked or on Sundays in the afternoon. She stood still long enough to comb her hair and count her money and that was the size of it.

There was one boarder who was definitely distracting. His name was George Batlin. No one could pronounce his Greek name so he had changed it when he came to America as a teenager. It seemed a good idea so that he could fit in to his new home, America.

George's brother owned a hardware store on Pennsylvania Avenue near the Capitol. George worked there as a stock boy and general helper. He was a clean boarder and paid his rent on time which definitely was a plus and attracted Mary. Besides he was so polite, it made Mary nervous.

One Sunday evening after lunch, George appeared at the kitchen door. "Miss Mary, may I visit with you?" Mary felt her face flush and felt a bit giddy and nervous. "Yes, she said, "come on in." As she washed dishes, he began to dry and stack them.

"On my day off, Sundays, I can help you here with fixing things that break and yard work," George said in slightly broken English." Mary certainly needed help with the yard and the many small projects she had been unable to tackle. He watched her and when she didn't respond he added, "I do good and you could think about giving me the room for the work I do for you." George added.

"No, we won't do that," Mary was quick to answer. "I

will pay you by the job" she responded. "You can start right now, Mr. Batlin, and clean up the yard for me." They agreed on a price and George worked in the yard the rest of the day. Mary was pleased. She asked Mr. Peavey to help her make a list of things she needed done and she would have it ready whenever George was available for more work. The arrangement worked out well. George was a hard worker and enjoyed Mary's company. He'd not seen many red haired ladies in his life and not met anyone sweeter or more hard working than Miss Mary. Their first kiss was a turning point in Mary's life. She had never really kissed a man before and it was awkward but in all ways for Mary, magical. Their relationship was slow to grow but grow it did. Six months passed quickly.

It was almost sundown and Mary was on the back porch finishing sweeping and readying for the next day's work.

George suddenly appeared behind her and as she turned to see who was there, he kissed her on the cheek. She stood there looking into his clear blue eyes and as if she had known exactly what to do, embraced him and their lips met. It wasn't so much the act of kissing that felt so natural, it was what Mary felt inside that filled her with a warmth and peace she had never known. It seemed their very souls touched and never wanted to let go. It was love and it was mutual.

Within three months, they were married. Before actually going through with it, Mary had to set one thing straight with George and it was a point that could end the relationship before it went any further.

She explained to George that she intended to keep the Boarding House in her name and that Mr. Peavey had a legal paper for George to sign before they married so in case it didn't last, Mary would keep her business. George agreed and they married on a Sunday in late August. George continued to work with his brother and to take care of all the maintenance at the Boarding House. Life was good and was as busy as ever for the two lovebirds.

CHAPTER 4

A year went by faster than the rest it seemed. Mary and George were a good team.

Mary had hired Mattie McGraw, a tiny and hard working Scottish widow to help with the cooking and housekeeping. Mattie was honest and dependable.

As time went by, George and Mary would set aside one Thursday a month, catch a train and go to the horse races in nearby towns like Bowie, Laurel, or Baltimore, Maryland. Mary loved the excitement of the races and had always loved horses. In her days of hopping freights, she and her brothers would go to Hagerstown and spend the day at the racetrack watching those beautiful horses run race after race. She also had a knack for picking winners. She had learned a megshift way of reading the racing form. Since numbers came easy, she'd match up the names of the horses as best she could and compare the paper to the program. It was the most fun Mary could ever remember and became a lifelong hobby and amusement. Mary could not help but notice right away that George had no head for gambling and would spend money without care or reason. Worse yet, he did not know when to stop. It was about a month after the racing season had ended that Mary realized there was a big problem brewing. George began to go on errands and not come back for hours. He became irritable and wanted money. He would tell Mary that his brother needed him to help at the store and not come home for days at a time.

Mary was no fool and had no patience with someone who could not tell the truth or control his habits. She gave George but one warning. She explained that she would not have any patience with a liar and a gambler and the next conversation on the subject would be the last. George promised on his Mother's grave his days of gambling were over.

A few weeks later, Mary took in a new boarder, Reverend Father Francis Malone. He would be staying only until the local church rectory was painted and repairs were made to the roof.

Father Malone loved Mary's cooking. Her corned beef and cabbage reminded him of his sainted Mother's. "Miss Mary," he said, "where are your little ones?" Mary replied, "Father, I am cursed as the doctor says I can have no babies of my own." "Pity of it all," he said, "I have watched you with the neighborhood children and you are a natural Mother."

It was just a few weeks later that Mary would receive

the most wonderful surprise of her life. Father Malone called Mary from the back yard to come to the front door. There in the hallway stood a tall, thin young man and woman. They looked frightened and nervous. "Mary, meet Mr. John Smith and Miss Jane." said Father. Mary shook the cold, clammy hand of John. His dark, close cropped hair, pale skin and sad expression caught Mary's attention. She looked at Jane, a plainly dressed, small blonde, blue-eyed bit of a girl. Jane was holding a baby, wrapped in a white blanket. The young girl's eyes began to well with tears.

Father Malone said, this baby needs you, Mary. These two had this baby girl out of wedlock and cannot keep her. Jane wants to go back to her family and cannot take the baby. I told them you would make an excellent Mother for this child and they want you to adopt her if you will," said Father Malone.

Mary was in shock and stood motionless for a minute or so and then said, "God must have meant this child for me and I will love her as if I was her natural Mother, I promise." Father Malone took the baby from Jane and gave her to Mary.

"We call her Dorothy," said Jane barely able to speak.

John cleared his throat and said, "If you will, I'd appreciate it if you would give her your choice of name and also name her Ellsworth."

Mary looked him straight in the eyes and understood his pain. She replied, "Her name will be Catherine Ellsworth

Batlin." Mary knew that George would approve as they had often wished for a little one of their own and she was hoping it would settle him into a more stable life. Mary quickly added, "I'll ask Mr. Peavey to have us some papers made to make this a legal act." She looked at the couple again and in her most serious tone said, "I do not want you two coming back sometime and wanting me to give this baby back to you or even to see her or we will not make this bargain." She added, "If you give her to me now, it will be for all time as if you never knew her so do we have a faithful deal or don't we?"

The couple agreed and came back the next day to sign the papers to that effect. Father Malone and Mattie were the witnesses and the papers were taken to the D. C. Courthouse where the case was sealed so that Catherine would never know any other parent. On the following Saturday, Catherine was christened with Father Malone giving a special blessing to the baby and her new parents. Mattie and Mr. Peavey were the proud Godparents.

The next few months were filled with adjustments for Mary, George, Mattie and the patrons of the boarding house. Mary and Mattie carried the load and Mary saw less and less of her husband. At first, she thought that the presence of little Catherine was unnerving to George. One evening, however, one of the boarders told Mary that he'd just left a card game where he and George were getting their pockets cleaned.

Mary's Irish temper was boiling in no time and by the

next morning when George was not at home when she awoke, she knew she had to face reality. George loved to gamble and that came first. George was about to be history and there wouldn't be any joy in it for Mary but it had to be done.

It was almost ten a.m. when Mary spotted George coming toward the back door. She grabbed a butcher knife from the rack and was waiting for him as he entered the kitchen.

"George, it's over for us and right now. I'm that mad at you. You had best pick up your things I've left for you just outside by the cellar door and never look back." George knew Mary was hell on wheels when she was angry and she was angry. He'd seen her take a tenant by the ear and then push him out the front door of the boarding house when the guy had been caught red handed stealing money from another tenant's room. When her temper was up, she'd take on the biggest of folks and cut them down to size. Before George could say anything, she squeezed out a final warning, "Don't even say a word, just turn around and go." She added, "If you come back here, you'll be dead and I'll be in jail. I'll cut out your gizzard and shove it in your eye." George knew he'd been a sorry husband and knew he didn't have a chance. He cleared the door and she never saw him again. She heard him say as he went for his clothes, "Take care of baby Catherine." "You bet your gambling ass I will," she yelled.

That afternoon, Mary asked Mr. Peavey to get their lawyer to draw up the papers and the divorce was a matter of time.

Mary knew that life would be hard for her alone but her mind was set. She went on as if George had never been in her life. She had no time for sadness or regrets. Seeing after Catherine and tending to business was an overwhelming task and as was her nature, Mary was head over heals into what had to be done. "One day at a time, sweet Jesus," Mary whispered as her feet hit the floor each morning. Mattie had not said much to Mary about all that had happened but did worry about her.

"Mary, you are losing too much weight and it worries me," said Mattie. "It takes a lean horse for a long race," replied Mary. Mattie then knew Mary would be fine as her strong will would carry her through tough times. Catherine was a happy, bright, and a good natured baby. At eleven months, she was walking and Mary kept a large homemade playpen in the kitchen so she could have Catherine with her as much as possible. Catherine loved the backyard and the old dog that had taken up there. Mattie was ever present, filling in whenever needed and was a blessing to both Mary and Catherine.

The next year went by as fast as the first and life at the Boarding House was pretty much a routine. Father Malone was no longer a boarder but saw Mary, Mattie, and Catherine each Sunday at church and stopped by for an occasional dinner.

CHAPTER 5

One Sunday afternoon, Father Malone stopped in to have his favorite, corned beef and cabbage, at no charge to him, of course. After he ate, he knocked on the kitchen door and asked Mary if he could have a moment of her time.

"Mary, the firehouse is having a grand celebration this coming Saturday." he said. They will be celebrating the completion of the new firehouse in the neighborhood, and I've been invited to give the benediction," said Father. "Mary, you need to get a day away from this place and I was wondering if you would accompany me there and also bring two of your pies with you?" he added.

Mary smiled as she thought over the offer. She said, "I'll ask Mattie to watch little Catherine and if she's willing, I'd be that proud to join you and bring the pies."

Mary looked forward to getting away from the Boarding House for a few hours. She had not visited often in the neighborhood and it would be good to meet some of her neighbors at the firehouse.

Father Malone was prompt in fetching Mary and quickly latched on to one of the pies and volunteered to carry both of them. There was a large gathering at the firehouse. Father Malone was introduced and asked to offer the Benediction. At the conclusion, he gave a short speech of welcome and introduced many of the neighbors including Mary. There was a time for all to gather and get acquainted and enjoy the food provided for the celebration. One young fireman was talking to Father Malone and soon they both approached Mary. The man was tall, had black wavy hair, dark brown eyes, and was as handsome a man as Mary had ever seen. Father Malone started to introduce them but the young man stepped forward saying, "Miss Mary, my name is James McDermott." Mary could feel her face flush but she managed a smile and made a sort of curtsy which made her feel all the more awkward. Father Malone stepped back and found his way over to the array of desserts for a slice of pie.

James continued, "Everybody here at the firehouse calls me Mack." She offered how happy she was to meet him and welcomed him to the neighborhood and hoped he liked his job. Mack said, "Father said you run the Flynn's Boarding House and you allow folks to stop by and have a meal if there's room at the table."

"Yes, Mack, you are welcome to join us when you can," said Mary. She tried her best to control the pitch of her voice but almost lost control as she added, "supper is served at five in the evening." The truth is both Mack and Mary were a bundle of nerves but managed to talk awhile. When he excused himself to answer a fire call, Mary wondered if she would ever see him again.

Three days went by routinely but on the next evening just a bit after five p.m., Mack was standing in the dining room looking for a place at the table. Mary spotted him and found a place she thought would do even though the room at the table seemed suddenly cramped. Mack dug right in and seemed to enjoy the pot roast, mashed potatoes, green beans, gravy and the banana pudding. After he'd had dessert, he asked Mary what she might be serving on Saturday evening as that would be his next evening off from the firehouse.

She could hardly breathe much less talk and mumbled, "Oh, I'll be looking forward to seeing you then." He came back all right and became a "regular" on the days he wasn't working at the "engine house" as Mack preferred to call it.

After a few months, they were friends exchanging stories and telling of daily events and sharing tales about their families. Mary felt so comfortable in his company. They would go out on the porch in the evening and Mary would take Catherine and they'd all swing in the glider until Catherine would fall asleep. Mack's Mother and sister lived in Cleveland Park, a neighborhood in the north part of the city, off Connecticut Avenue. His father had been a fireman and was killed in a hotel fire when Mac was a small boy. His mother was a devout Catholic and Mac worried about her as she was always praying and fasting to the point she would become ill and end up confined to bed. The doctor warned her that her faith would carry her away some day. His sister, Nadie, was still at home, and though she worked at the AT&T phone Company, she was there in the evenings to care for her Mother. Mack told Mary that it was all too much for him and he only visited when he felt a need to check on them. He knew that his Mother would not approve of him in the company of a woman who had her own business, had been divorced, and had a child so the subject was not discussed.

Mack had a room over the garage of a friend and fellow fireman, Sam Rayburn. Since the firemen worked two days on and two days off, there wasn't much need to have more than a clean bed and place for his clothing so the arrangement worked well for Mack. He did talk about having his own home someday and a family too. Mary thought that was a very nice plan. In fact, she could feel herself drawn in to a plan like that and spent some time daydreaming about what it would be like to be in a family again, her family. She would love to have a flower and vegetable garden, time to tend the roses, and take Catherine for long walks or to the zoo. She cringed at the thought of finding another husband like George though. After all, she had thought George would be kind, sweet, and hard working but all of that part of their marriage soon disappeared. Maybe it just wasn't meant to be for her. Life was too filled with everyday tasks for Mary to spend much time thinking about such complicated dreams.

Catherine was a quiet, cheerful child. She could be seen following Mary or Mattie throughout each day. She loved it outdoors best. If one of the ladies was on a porch or in the yard, Catherine was there. Her only playmate was her dog, Zip. She loved to talk to the boarders and as she grew older, wandered about the boarding house freely as she was not a child to create messes or play with things once told to leave them alone She was content to play with Zip, her jump rope, jacks, and her favorite, a china doll, a gift from Mack. Mr. Peavey took time to teach Catherine her A,B,C"s and often read to her in the evenings. Mary or Mattie took Catherine to the park on Saturday. In the heat of summer, Catherine joined the other neighborhood children playing in the fountains that lay between Union Station and the U.S. Capitol building. Underpants was the swimwear of the day and Catherine loved being with the other children.

It was about this time Brother Dave wrote he would be marrying a Martinsburg girl, Wilda King. Dave had returned home from the War and found Wilda to be the most beautiful and gentle girl he'd met. She was talented too and could crochet and made her own clothing. She was shy and barely spoke but loved to spend time with him and agreed to become Mrs. David Flynn. A few months later, Dave visited Mary explaining the marriage was short lived. On their honeymoon a dreadful thing had happened. Wilda suddenly became violent when it was time for their first night together. Dave later found out that Wilda had been raped as a small child by a neighbor boy and the reality of the event did not register until her wedding night. Wilda became reclusive, talked to what appeared to be ghosts, repeatedly ran away and had screaming fits. The lovely young girl was soon admitted to the West Virginia Asylum for the Insane. Dave was told that State Law read that he could not obtain a divorce as long as Wilda was declared insane or until her death. The Flynn family had not had to bear such sad circumstances since the loss of their baby brother. Dave was devastated at the loss of his true love. He could not go back to Martinsburg and decided to look for work in Washington. He landed a job in nearby Virginia as a fireman thanks to Mack who had a friend at the Virginia Fire Department. Dave shared stories of Wilda from time to time. Some twenty years later Wilda underwent successful treatments which would allow her to leave the asylum and Dave was able to obtain a divorce.

Fashions were also changing. Mary noticed the ladies of fashion were binding their breasts and wearing short dresses. She and Mattie decided it was time to keep up with style as they were in the public too. One Saturday afternoon, they talked one of the fashion minded lady boarders into sharing the fashion secrets of the day and soon the two of them were happily modern with flat, bound, bosoms, and no noticeable waists. Their hair was cut into short bobs, they sent for some new fashions from the Sears Catalog and they looked like the rest of the "flappers" of the day.

Mack took notice too and told Mary he thought she looked a lot like movie star, Lillian Gish. He wasn't sure he liked her binding her breasts but decided that some things were best left unsaid. Mary was even more taken with him for noticing and invited him to take her to the races the next time he had a day free from work.

The next weekend Mack and Mary headed for Laurel Race Track in Mack's new Ford coupe. Mary couldn't believe how extra special it was to be taken to her very favorite horse races in a new automobile by one of the most handsome men she'd ever known. Even more outstanding, it was her very first ride in a new automobile. The experience almost left her speechless. She thought, this may not be heaven, but it must be the next best thing! Mack tried his best to be at ease through the whole experience, but he couldn't help but laugh out loud when Mary began to touch the door, the seats, and the dash, asking what each knob and button was for, and exactly how the car was able to go and stop. The experience was a joy for both of them.

What a day! Mack had never been to a horse race. He was impressed with how much Mary seemed to know about the races, betting, and even winning. Mary explained that as a child, she and her brothers would hop a freight car to Charlestown or Hagerstown and spend as much time as possible watching the horse races and talking to the people there. Mack had won five dollars on a two dollar bet and he was hooked. That was easy money and he was having the best time. By the end of the day, Mack had won seven dollars and Mary had won twelve. On the trip home, they stopped at the Dixie Pig B-B-Q Restaurant. Mary had not eaten a barbeque sandwich before and asked to go in to the kitchen to talk to the cook. She wanted to know how to make that wonderful barbeque and serve it at the boarding house.

Mack began coming to see Mary every evening when he was not working. Sometimes Mary would put him to work or just talk to him while she worked. It seemed as though there just weren't enough hours in the day to do all that needed to be done. Business was good, but the routine was getting the best of Mary. After five years of really hard work, Mary began to long for a better life for her and Catherine.

CHAPTER 6

It was September 20, 1921, Catherine's fifth birthday. Dinner at the Boarding House was special that evening. Mary had baked a huge chocolate sheet cake and Pierre had stopped by to decorate it. Happy Birthday, Catherine, was scrolled on it and he'd drawn a little girl and a dog playing with a ball just below five blue candles. Catherine was so excited she began to sing to herself, "Happy Birthday to me" and the entire dinner crowd joined in signing with her. She kissed and hugged Pierre who blushed with pride. Mack brought Catherine a pink teddy bear. Catherine gave him a big hug and told him it was her very favorite color and that she would take good care of Teddy. Mary had made vanilla ice cream and the party was one Catherine remembered all her life.

That evening Mary and Mack found time to sit on the swing on the front porch. Mack said, "Mary, I have been told that I will be changing jobs and will be sent to the engine house on Connecticut Avenue in January. I'm going to drive the hook and ladder and I'll be making more money. Mary, have you ever thought about marrying again?" Before Mary could say a word, Mack said, "Mary, will you marry me?" Mary was taken aback and for a time words failed her.

"Mack, I do love you and you are a fine man, but that's a lot to throw on a girl and I do need time to think about it." She explained, "I have this place here, Catherine, and Mattie to think about. I don't know how I could make you a good wife and do all that too."

Mary was just talking out loud as though she was trying to solve her own problems as she talked, which was something she had always done.

She continued, "Catherine will start school next year and I promised Father Malone I'd raise her Catholic so I have to make sure she is in a Catholic School." She then added, "I'm getting too tired to keep up this pace and I would love to sell it all and just go live in a quiet place where Catherine could grow up playing with other children and I could visit with the family and have a nice home for my husband and me." She hesitated, "Mack, I think you are the right man for me as you are quiet, decent, a good Catholic man, and you treat me fine. You don't say much and whatever I want seems fine with you so, yes, I do want to be your wife, Mack." Catching her breath again, "I'll settle down in a minute Mac, and before you take back your offer, I say YES, I will!"

Mack felt as if he'd been run over by a fire engine and

was almost speechless.

He said, "I'll come by tomorrow, Mary, and be sure you won't be changing your mind."

They said goodnight and for the first time, Mack kissed her and held her close. Mary dropped in the swing and continued to sit there for quite a while. Her mind was numb with happiness and fear as well. What had she said? Where did all those feelings come from all at once and just what did she think she was doing? She had always been in control of Mary, just the way she liked it. She thought about Mack and what joy he'd brought to her life. She didn't even really know what he was like. She knew he was quiet and mannerly. She knew he was good to Catherine and had a Mother and Sister and that he was a fireman. She knew Father Malone liked him and that was the extent of it.

She did more than like him. He was everything most women look for in a man. He was gentle, kind, handsome, and well-mannered, had a good job, and did what he set out to do. Her heart took over and she knew what she wanted. It was to be Mrs. James Hugh McDermott.

About that time, Mattie came looking for Mary. Mattie said, "Mary I finished the dishes and set the table for breakfast, have the coffee pots ready, the ham sliced, the sheets folded, and…Mary, are you all right?"

"Sit down, Mattie, I need to talk to you," said Mary. Mattie sat down and sighed, "Lordy, I'm give out." Mary looked at her, "Mattie, what if I told you, I'm in love with Mack." "No surprise to me", said Mattie. Mary touched her hand, "Mattie what if I said I'm going to marry him and sell the boarding house." Mattie put her hand on Mary's head, "no fever, I guess you are at yourself."

Mary stood up, "Mattie, I'm not joking; I've been thinking about a world of things, this place, Catherine, you, me and Mack." She sighed and said, "I've been thinking of the years here and that I'm getting tired of this life and how it will be for Catherine to grow up here and I want her to have a real home, playmates, and a good Mammy and Papa.."

Mattie smiled, "Mary, I've been with you for many years now and I've been putting my money by for the time so I could have a place like this."

She said, "I bet you noticed that I've been sweet on that dear man, Henry Peavey for a very long time, but I don't think you know he also cares for me."

Now standing, Mattie said, "I would like to buy this place when you are ready to sell it, Mary, if the price is right."

Mary could not believe what she had just heard. That would solve one of her biggest hurdles. Mary smiled and declared, "Mattie, you are more than a friend to me, you are an angel from heaven above, and no, I didn't know Mr. Peavey was that fond of you, you sly one."

They giggled and hugged and promised to talk more tomorrow about the deal.

CHAPTER 7

Mack and Mary set the date, November 4, the first Saturday in November. Mr. Peavey and the lawyer would work out the transfer of the boarding house to Mattie by then. The couple set out to find a home for the three of them. It had to be near the engine house on Connecticut Avenue, be near enough to a school for Catherine, and be pleasing to all of them. Mary told Mack she would like to find a place big enough to accommodate "roomers" to help with their expenses and also to give Mary her own way to supplement their income. Her independence would not die with the marriage. Mack agreed to most everything Mary wanted as it was his nature and he did not like disagreements.

Within a few weeks they found a two story home just off Wisconsin Avenue, north of Tenleytown. There was one bedroom on the first floor, a sitting room which would become Catherine's bedroom, a bathroom, lovely living room with a fireplace, and a large kitchen with room for a dining table. Upstairs, there were two bedrooms, a bathroom, and storeroom. The basement held storage space, a coal furnace, a two wash tubs. The sellers were also willing to part with some beautiful old furniture at a most reasonable price. It was perfect and they all settled in and enjoyed their first Christmas as a real family in a real family home.

Mary rented the two rooms to two nice young men who were also firemen and would be great roomers since they would be doing "shift work" like Mac and be gone forty-eight hours at a time. The next year, Catherine started first grade at the nearby Catholic school and Mary thoroughly enjoyed her home and family. She had her flower and vegetable gardens and time for family. The years passed pleasantly and Mary watched Catherine grow into a beautiful young lady. Catherine was taught to wash, sew, and care for a home. With these additional chores, Catherine didn't spend much time in the kitchen and never really developed a desire to cook. She admired the way Mary could whip up some of the most amazing and tasty meals and was content to leave that to her Mother. Try as Mary would, she could never find the words to tell Catherine she had been adopted and over the years, had decided to leave well enough alone. Sadly, one day when Catherine was twelve and had disobeyed her mother causing Mary to cry, Mack lost his temper, and in an unusual fit of anger, told Catherine she had been adopted. It was a crushing blow to Catherine and to Mary. Whatever disobedience caused the outburst was quickly overcome by the revelation. Mary explained to Catherine that even though she was not her own flesh and blood, she loved her even more and had chosen her to love forever as a gift from God Himself. She told Catherine that she had been married to George then but did not tell Catherine the details of how she came to become her Mother. She went on to say she had the court case sealed to protect both Catherine and her real parents from any future hurtful problems. Catherine was overcome with emotion at first and never fully forgave Mack for telling her in such a heated way as it had cut through to her very soul. It was the first real crisis the family had shared. Time and love helped the pain go away and Catherine knew how much she was loved but part of her always wanted to know who her parents were and what circumstances caused them to give her away.

In 1927 the economy was becoming unstable and presented the next big crisis for not only the McDermott family but the nation. Prices for goods and services continued to climb. The stock market crashed the following year and the nation was in turmoil.

Many folks were homeless, slept in parks and in barns. The hungry stood in long lines in front of soup kitchens run by churches and charities like the Salvation Army.

Some of the firemen lost their jobs and the rest had to settle for lower pay and times were getting tough. As the next few years passed, the economy worsened. The roomers moved out. Mary had to find ways to save every penny. She planted a larger garden using seeds she had saved from the prior summer. She took in new roomers for whatever they could pay.

Mary recalled she had to quit school at an early age and Catherine had just completed her freshman year at Sacred Heart Catholic School. They needed another income. Mary asked Father Malone to put in a good word for her and she secured a job cleaning the school cafeteria after the luncheon meal. She carefully saved every penny and used every resource she had to keep the family going. Two years passed and things weren't getting any better for the family. Mary was near exhaustion and Mack told her that she must quit the job at the school. It was time for Catherine to leave school and go to work to help out. That sounded like a good idea to Catherine who had grown tired of school but vowed to get her diploma someday. She was ready to get a job. If she got a job, she would have to stop going by the corner drug store for a candy bar and to flirt with the soda jerk, Vernon Parker. As it worked out Vernon was changing jobs.

That just made the two young couple do all they could to remain connected to one another. He was really keen and she knew he was sweet on her too.

The next door neighbor was employed at Lansburg's Department Store. Mary knocked on her door one Saturday, "Mrs. Hurt, I want to ask you how my Catherine might find employment at Lansburg's." Mrs. Hurt was fond of Catherine and inquired what would cause Catherine to want a job at age sixteen? Mary explained that hard times had caused the need and Mrs. Hurt agreed to help. The next day, Catherine was called in for an interview and hired as an elevator operator.

In no time, Catherine's good manners and wholesome good looks had attracted the buyer in Ladies Hats and Fine Clothing and Catherine was given some modeling jobs at the store. She was quite willing to do whatever jobs they gave her and she became well liked.

Mrs. Taylor, the Assistant Manager in the Hat and Fine Clothing Department asked Catherine to be at the Palace Theater on the first Saturday in December that year to represent the store in a beauty contest. The star of the show and judge of the contest would be none other than Eddie Cantor, the famous singer and comedian. Catherine was given a bathing suit to wear as were all the other contestants and Mr. Cantor came backstage before the show started to meet the girls and explain how they were to enter the stage and what to say as he talked to each one during the show. They were instructed to walk across the stage one at a time and stop beside Mr. Canter and hold his hand until he released theirs and then proceed in the same direction until they were off stage. He would be singing "IF YOU KNEW SUSIE". At the end of the show he would call all of them back and they would enter, stage left, in a line. At that time he would choose the second runner up, first runner up, and contest winner. The winner would be given a trip to Hollywood and a screen test. Catherine was first runner up and received a bouquet and $25. It was easy to see why she'd done so well. At five foot six, she was slim, graceful and shapely. Her dark brown hair was slightly wavy and neatly groomed bringing attention to her lively blue eyes, delicate Roman nose, creamy ivory complexion, and continuous smile. She certainly was pretty enough to be a movie star. The department store was thrilled and each time Catherine did modeling jobs, she was introduced as the first runner up in the Palace Theater Beauty Contest throughout the following year. Needless to say, Mary was proud though she had not approved of Catherine participating in the contest but was happy to see the $25.

There were very few things to be happy about in 1932. The Stock Market was struggling and times were more than hard. Many banks had closed and savings were lost. Mary had put some money in Postal Savings and it was safe but she decided to leave it alone in case of emergency. Mack didn't even know she had the money and that was not by design, just part of Mary's nature to put money aside. Mack was still working as a fireman and had enough seniority to hold him there for awhile anyway. His salary was cut drastically though. Food continued to be hard to come by at any reasonable price. Mary often went to the grocery store and asked for the damaged and bruised fruit and vegetables that had been set aside for the garbage. The produce man would give it to her and she'd bring it home, clean it, and salvage what she could. She tried to get enough of the vegetables and fruits to make it worthwhile canning. Any amount was good for something as Mary didn't waste anything. That was another life-long habit. Mack and many other men found themselves riding to work on bicycles, hitching rides or walking to work. He'd even walked those four miles to work when there was no other way. Times were horrible and everyone shared the misery. President Roosevelt had started The New Deal and slowly people were starting back to work. There was some hope that better times were coming but rationing was continuing.

Throughout those years Catherine found time and ways to keep in touch with Vernon. Mary insisted that Catherine date other nice young men, ones she thought might have money or good enough jobs to give Catherine a better life. Of course, Catherine did try to please her Mama, but she didn't find anyone quite as keen as Vernon. Catherine had some really bad experiences with boys her Mother had recommended and considered worthy of her. She got Mary's attention one night when she came home walking by herself with a torn blouse after refusing advances from one of Mary's choice dates. After a full year of trying to please her Mother, Catherine decided to follow her heart. Vernon asked Mary and

Mack for Catherine's hand in marriage and they reluctantly gave their blessing.

    Catherine and Vernon were a great match. Catherine continued to work at Lansburg's and Vernon worked for Capitol Transit Company driving a bus. They had a one bedroom apartment on Harrison Street not all that far from Mary and Mac. During the four years that followed, life was almost uneventful except for one miscarriage along the way. Catherine and Vernon were so happy that chilly day in March, 1940 when they stopped by to share their good news with Mary. Catherine was pregnant again. Mary was more than thrilled and secretly hoped Catherine would have a little girl. Vernon had his wishes too and it was for a boy. He needed a fishing buddy and that's all he talked about. On Catherine's twenty-third birthday, a baby girl, Mary Catherine was born in Georgetown Hospital. Mary was beside herself with joy and even gave Vernon a big hug and kiss.

    Vernon told Catherine he hoped little Cathie would love to go fishing with him and it turned out she did. By that time, World War Two was in the news and all young men were either volunteering or being drafted. Vernon was drafted and went off to war in the Pacific. He was twenty six, old by Army standards, was color blind and flat footed. He was assigned to the Infantry and was taught to repair Piper Cub aircraft. Vernon tried to write as often as possible but he was constantly on the move. Right after boot camp he was put on a train along with what he thought was most of the Army and stood up all the way from Washington, D. C. to Monterey, California. Sleeping and eating was done leaning on other soldiers and taking turns in seats.

He was immediately put on a troop carrier, an old converted supply ship. Hammocks were hung three high in long rows and troops took turns working and sleeping through the long and slow voyage. In those crowded quarters, the men did the best they could to just survive the ordeal of ship life in all the poorest circumstances. Vernon was in New Guinea, Guam, Borneo and the Philippines. When the war was over, Vernon returned home with a case of Malaria but was soon back with the family in one piece and in most ways healthy.

Soon after Vernon left for the war, Mary and Mack found a wonderful home in Bethesda, at 4828 Leland Street, where they would spend the rest of their lives together. Again, there were rooms to rent and Mary continued to collect extra money.

Cathie, their new granddaughter, was a colicky, restless, disagreeable bundle of trouble. Catherine didn't know much about how to care for a baby, especially a troubled one. Sue, Mary's sister, was recently widowed and was willing to move in for a while and help out. Sister, Lucy, also visited often and tried her hand. There was no doubt that Catherine could use help. Cathie cried enough for ten babies and no amount of food, cuddling, singing, or cussing seemed to help. The reason was colic and there just wasn't an easy cure for it. One lovely October evening, Lucy took Cathie out on the porch in the moonlight to quiet the colicky baby. She was heard to say as she rocked the child, "See the moon, see the moon, see the God Damned Moon!" Time and medicine for colic finally quieted Cathie, but left the entire family wondering if God made many like her. Since Vernon had gone overseas, Catherine realized she could not keep the apartment. Catherine and Cathie moved in with Mary and Mack

Catherine secured a job as a file clerk with the Navy Department. The home on Leland Street was also a two-story bungalow. As fortune would have it one of Mary's roomers moved and Mary gave one bedroom to Catherine and Cathie. Catherine worked in a temporary building by the Reflecting Pool in front of the Lincoln Memorial. Mary kept Cathie during the day. Mac and Mary enjoyed Cathie most of the time. They had a pet name for her. It was Dumpling. Somehow, over the year, it was shortened to Dump.

Mary was in her fifties and had gained considerable weight. Her flattened bosoms were now large, elephant ear like appendages which fell beneath her waist when let out of her brassiere. Mac was still relatively slim and strong as his profession required he be in good physical condition but his hair was streaked with more gray than black and his energy level had diminished to the point that Mary kept after him to finish his yard work, put his tools away, and make household repairs. Also, with Catherine and Cathie as full-time residents, life had become a lot busier than the couple had experienced in years.

During this time, Washington, D. C. was subject to air raid warnings and blackout times as World War II affected everyone. Many of the warnings were posted in the newspaper so that residents would know how to react to them. Not all warnings were announced. When the air raid horns were sounded, all residents were to turn out all lights, shut all curtains and remain silent until the "all clear" signal was sounded. If on the road, all vehicles were to turn off lights and stop safely and quickly. All businesses were to follow the same rules. So as not to scare Cathie, the family made a game of it telling Cathie to be quiet and wait until she heard the angel's horn.

CHAPTER 8

Cathie had learned to walk at ten months and talk earlier than most babies thanks to so many adults in her young life. By age three, Cathie was a bundle of curiosity and innocent mischief. She was almost more than Mary wanted to handle and by the end of each day Mary was exhausted. Cathie could ask more questions than any one human could answer. She tried to involve Mary in every minute of her waking day and she drove Mary to distraction at mealtime. Cathie was never interested in eating any meal. She had no favorite foods, not even sweet ones. Each meal was a test of wills and Mary did all she could to coax Cathie to eat almost anything. Because "Dump" was not eating properly the inevitable bowl problems were just another continuous battle. Mary would struggle with a squirming child and a bottle of milk of magnesia or when all else failed, the dreaded enema. It was hard to love such a child!

One morning was exceptionally memorable following

an enema treatment. Cathie was still full of energy after the morning ordeal and spilled her coffee flavored milk all over her dress. Cathie had just finished eating half of an onion and mayonaise sandwich since that's all that had appealed to her that entire morning. It was almost lunch time. At wits end, Mary washed her, dressed her in fresh underwear and told Cathie it was nap time. She marched Cathie up the stairs, pulled the drapes, tucked a restless child in bed and told her to lay still and take a nap or she was going to get a "fanning" and Mary didn't mean MAYBE!

Cathie just couldn't seem to rest. She looked all around the room for a stray toy but didn't find one, peeked out the window to find some amusement in the yard below but nothing was stirring, so she hopped back up on the bed, grabbed hold of the lamp on the nightstand, unscrewed the light bulb, turned on the switch, licked her finger and put it in the socket. Cathie fell back on the bed, the lamp hit the floor, and Mary went running up the stairs only to find one limp little girl out cold on the bed. She checked her breathing. Thank the Lord, she was breathing and soon was conscious. Mary looked at the lamp without the bulb, still plugged in to the wall and realized that the little girl could have killed herself. "Oh, Ganna, I scared myself." Cathie began to cry and then Mary began to cry. What would happen if the child had killed herself. Mary quickly decided they both needed a nap. "Oh, God, protect me in days like this." Mary prayed as she drifted off to sleep.

Mac and Uncle Earl decided to build a playhouse for Cathie in the backyard. Some good soul had given scrap wood and other building materials to Earl in payment for a painting a home. The two had the small playhouse finished in record time and it was as adorable as any playhouse ever created out of scraps. In fact, Mary couldn't believe how well the men had done especially without the experience she knew they lacked. The little square house was under a pyramid type roof. They had added a little porch with a bench on each side of the Dutch style doors. There were two tiny windows overlooking the porch and a window on each side and back of the little square building. The roof was shingled. The clapboard siding was painted white and the benches and trim were in a medium shade of blue. Mary had found a child's used table and two chairs for sale at the Farmer's Market. She also found a set of children's dishes at the Five & Dime Store and placed them on the little shelves built in to the playhouse interior walls. She sewed curtains out of scrap material and hung them with pieces of elastic and thumb tacks.

    Cathie was beside herself with joy. She took her dolly and dolly bed to her playhouse and Mary gave her a small old bathroom rug for the floor. They cut off a broom to make it fit Cathie's size for sweeping the playhouse and Cathie was happy at play there most every day. She invited playmates Martha Hickerson, Linda Waterfield, and the twins, Rosemary and Ramona to come and play and have tea parties. The playhouse was a magical place for all the little girls on Leland Street and Cathie was happy to share it.

That Easter Mary had been given a pair of chickens, a Bandy Hen and Rooster by Florence's daughter, Doris. Cathie named them Molly and Dick after characters in one of the books Catherine had often read to her at bedtime. Molly and Dick had the run of the yard and Mary had plucked their tail feathers to make sure they could not fly away. They were used to Cathie and she would often feed them from her hand. They would also join her running in and out of the water sprinkler as she played on hot, summer days. They were put in a coop in the evening and all the family was enjoying their feathered pets.

Cathie was in the backyard with the chickens one day when the old cat who lived a few doors away decided to go chicken hunting. Suddenly Dick flew up and onto the back of the cat that had crouched near the hydrangea bush at the corner of the yard. The cat took off over the fence with Dick still on board. It could have ended badly but Mary went over the fence to fetch Dick and soon the chickens were in someone else's barnyard as Mary vowed never to hop another fence. The fence had to be repaired and Mary's bruises left a lasting reminder for most of the month.

If things weren't jumping in the backyard, they would fire up in the front yard. Cathie did have a playmate just next door and that was Martha Hickerson. She was a pretty little brunette and also an only child. Her mother and father doted on Martha much the same as Cathie's family did her. Both girls were strong willed. One day, Martha wanted to ride Cathie's tricycle and Cathie gave in. When she felt Martha had been riding long enough, she asked her to give back the tricycle. Martha resisted and Cathie tried to physically remove her from her tricycle. In the scuffle, Martha bit Cathie on the wrist and Cathie ran in to show her Ganna. Mary told Cathie to go out there and bite Martha and retrieve her tricycle. Cathie bolted out the front door to do just that and Mary watched. Of course, Martha was not about to allow Cathie to bite her and furthermore, she was enjoying the tricycle and would not get off without a fight. The girls were causing a roar on the sidewalk and both Mrs. Hickerson and Mary were right there in a flash. Mary told Mrs. Hickerson that Martha had bitten Cathie and demanded that Cathie have the opportunity to show Martha how it felt to be bitten. Mrs. Hickerson grabbed her precious daughter and headed for the house. Mary chased after them with her fist in the air, telling them to stay off her property until Martha was ready to apologize and ready to be bitten.

    Mary was never fond of Mrs. Hickerson after that day. She told Catherine and Mack what had happened at the dinner table that evening. She remarked that Mrs. Hickerson looked like a Pussy Willow, so tall and thin with curly white hair in little puffs all over her head. After that when she talked about

Mrs. Hickerson for any reason, she referred to her as Pussy Willow. A few months later, Mary had more words with Mrs. Hickerson, over the fence. "Look, Pussy Willow, I want to warn you to stop taking the ripe figs from my fig tree as I don't get enough for canning." said Mary. Mrs. Hickerson tried to explain she only took the ones that were over in her yard but Mary just became more angry and Mrs. Hickerson, by then in tears, turned and ran to the house. Needless to say, Mrs. Hickerson avoided being in the yard when Mary was anywhere in sight and she probably wondered why Mary had called her Pussy Willow.

One hot July day, Mary took Cathie to the second floor bathroom to bathe her. Mary filled the tub with a shallow amount of warm water, placed Cathie in the tub and realized that she had forgotten the shampoo. "Don't move for any reason", Mary explained, while I get the shampoo I left downstairs." As soon as Cathie was sure Mary was at the bottom of the stairs, she got out of the tub and locked the bathroom door with the skeleton key she found in the lock and returned to the tub. When Mary topped the stairs and saw the door closed, she knew she was in for trouble. She tried to open the door and realized it must be locked. "Dump, open the door," she shirked. Cathie got out of the tub and tried to unlock the door. Mary told Cathie to shove the key under the door so that she could unlock it. Cathie took the key out of the lock and pushed it under the door. That was impossible as the door jam prevented that from happening. Cathie could not slip the key under the door and Mary could not retrieve it. Cathie began to cry.

"You'll cry when I get in there," yelled Mary. "Now wrap yourself in that towel and sit on the rug until I get in there and DON'T TOUCH ANYTHING or I'll skin you for sure," Mary said breathlessly. Mary had few choices. She could force open the door and probably break it and even hurt Cathie in the process. She could get the ladder and climb up on the roof over the garage, open the window and crawl through it; she could call Mack home to help her but that would take at least an hour or more or she could get a neighbor but probably wouldn't find a man at home at midday. There was only one thing to do, get the ladder.

Mary went down to the basement, fetched the ladder and up on the roof she went, moving as fast as a gal a quarter her age. She made it to the window and hoped that window was not locked. She raised it carefully and started in. She had no trouble getting her head and shoulders in, the bosom was somewhat of a problem but the hips were just too wide for entry. For a moment or two, Mary was wedged. Cathie huddled in her towel awaiting her fate. Mary backed out of the window and down the ladder she came, madder than a hornet. Her red hair was standing on end, her face as red as a ripe tomato, sweat poured down her face and neck. She was shaking so hard she could barely think. She ran out to the front of the house in a panic and spied the milkman's truck about to stop in front of her home.

"Help me, Help me", she cried. Mary grabbed him by the arm and said, "You are the one I need."

The bewildered milkman followed as Mary explained her dilemma. He climbed the ladder, crawled through the window and found the key and opened the door. Cathie was snatched up in a bundle by Mary. She thanked the milkman and offered him a small reward which he refused. She was left holding that incorrigible child. It just wasn't always easy to love this one. Still shaking and sweating Mary waited a while for her blood pressure to return to normal before she was able to speak.

She ran fresh warm water in the tub and explained to Cathie why what she had done was such a very bad thing. Cathie didn't need an explanation this time as she had experienced the most fear a child could absorb in one day and live through it. Seeing Mary come through the window, get stuck, and vanish and then contemplate the consequences of her actions had left a lasting impression on Dump. This was one of the few times Cathie was able to escape normal punishment, a trip to the willow tree to choose a switch for a much deserved spanking. Mary was just too exhausted and both enjoyed a long nap.

CHAPTER 9

That next summer, Cathie was playing in the backyard and wandered behind the playhouse where Mack kept his pile of firewood for winter. There, not quite in plain sight, was a large, dead rat. Not knowing about such things, it looked about the size of Cathie's favorite dolly. She poked it and it didn't move. She petted it and it felt soft. It looked as though it was sleeping. Cathie picked it up, took it to her playhouse and dressed it in a pink dolly dress with matching bonnet. She then wrapped it in a blanket. To her joy, the neighbors were talking over the back fence to Mrs. Hickerson next door. Cathie hurried over to show the neighbors her new "baby". They looked horrified and asked her where she got it and told her not to play with it and to tell her Grandma. About that time, Mary appeared at the back door of the screened porch to call Cathie in for the afternoon. Cathie turned and walked toward her Grandma, smiling and eager to share her new "dolly" asleep in the blanket. Mary looked down at the rat and almost passed out. She turned bright red and screamed, "DROP THAT RAT THIS MINUTE!"

Cathie dropped the rat and it lay there serenely in dress and bonnet. Mary started toward the fence where the neighbors were still visiting with one another. Mary was beet red and her hair looked to be on fire. Her feet were moving as if she was stomping grapes; her arms were waving all about.

She screamed, "YOU IDIOTS! DID YOU SEE THAT CHILD WITH THAT DEAD RAT? WHY I OUGHT TO COME OVER THIS FENCE AFTER ALL OF YOU!" She whirled around, grabbed Cathie and headed for the house. Cathie was taken directly to the cellar, placed in the wash tub, stripped, and washed with Lava soap until she thought her skin would rub away completely. "Rough Ganna," she cried.

Mary dried her, dressed her, told her about dead rats and all the germs and plagues they carry and sent the child to the willow tree to get a switch. It was one of those days that Cathie will remember all her life. It could be that the neighbors would recount that tale for years to follow as well.

Through the years the adventures continued. Mary and Cathie often walked to Wisconsin Avenue shopping at the Farmer's Market, grocery, hardware, and the many stores lining the avenue. One day, Mary took Cathie to the A & P Grocery and told her to sit up front on a bench where she could watch out the window and watch the cashiers as they worked while Mary shopped.

"Dump, I'll only be gone a little while and I don't want you to go anywhere so just sit here", she warned. Looking over her shoulder, Mary said, "Promise me you won't leave the store." Cathie promised.

Time went by and Ganna was nowhere in sight. Cathie inched her way along the bench so that she could glance down the aisles but could not see her Grandmother. She did it again and again and decided that her Grandma must have forgotten her. She began to think about what she'd do if she were lost or alone. That was something she and Catherine had talked about once and Catherine had told her not to talk to strangers, only policemen. Not lacking in imagination, the five year old, decided she should look again for Ganna, aisle by aisle. She did not find her. Cathie decided it was time to take herself to the Police Station, also on Wisconsin Avenue. Since she knew where that was, she headed out the door in that direction. The station was four blocks north on the same side of the avenue. At each street, she waited for the others pedestrians to cross and she followed at the same time. During the walk, Cathie continued to look in all directions hoping to spot her Ganna. In no time, she was walking up the stairs to the Police Department. A policeman was coming out and that was good as Cathie could have never opened the huge door by herself. She explained to the policeman at the desk that her Grandma told her to wait on a bench at the A & P and never came back to get her a long, long, long time ago.

"What's your name?" the officer inquired.

"Cathie, but you can call me Dump, that's what my Ganna calls me," she said.

"What's your last name?" he asked. "

It's Parker but that's not my Ganna's name," Cathie offered.

"What's her name?" the officer continued.

"Mary and she lives with Mack," Cathie responded.

About that time, Mary came thundering through the door. She was visibly shaken, out of breath, and flushed.

"Dump!" she exclaimed. The policeman asked Cathie if that was her Grandmother but Cathie did not answer. She threw herself into Mary's arms and large tears flowed from her eyes. Grandma cried as well and was given a glass of water as she appeared about to be faint. The policeman complimented Mary on having taught her granddaughter what to do if she was lost. Mary was too relieved to find Cathie to really tell the policeman what she thought of the entire situation. Later, Mary told Cathie that if she ever disobeyed her again, she would use every branch of the willow tree on her. Cathie tried to explain why she left the store, but her words fell on deaf ears.

Mary had never lost her love for the horse races. When Mack had the day off from work, he would drive the car to the local racetracks and of course, Cathie went along too.

Cathie loved the excitement of the races and being close

to the beautiful horses. The local tracks were small and Mary would allow Cathie to go down and buy a hot dog or go to the paddock before a race and talk to the horses and jockeys. When Mack had to work, the girls would go to the races by train. That was Cathie's favorite way to travel. They would go to Laurel, or Hagerstown, Maryland, Charlestown, West Virginia and sometimes to Baltimore, Maryland, spending the day at Pemlico Race Track. Cathie loved going to Laurel best. It was a friendly place where she met Fats, the bookie, and the priests who would sit with him on folding chairs down by the rail and in front of the grandstand. Fats was an enormous and jolly man. Everyone liked him and Cathie was no exception. She'd ask him which horse was going to win the next race and if he told her, she'd run back to Mary with the latest tip. Cathie enjoyed watching Mary during a race. Mary would really get excited and jump up and down. She'd roll up the racing form and beat the rail with it, yelling, "Come on, come on, you can do it" or whatever she felt like screaming as she encouraged her horse. If she won, she'd jump around and head for the payout booth to claim her winnings. Later in life, Mary and Mack would buy two young thoroughbreds only to lose them in a "Claims race". Mrs. Bean, one of Mary's racing friends told Mary that her nephew was looking for a buyer for two young male horses that had never raced but had good blood lines. Mary told Mack it had been her life long dream to own her own horse. The price was within their range and they made the deal. During the second visit to see the young steeds, Mary noticed a thin band around the horses' hips. Attached to it was ring which fitted over their "studly" anatomy. She just had to know what that apparatus was supposed to do for the horses. The trainer explained that the confined horses often entertained themselves by swinging their penises from side to side, a horse's way of playing with himself. When this happened, the horse was less likely to put forth his best effort in a race. If confined in the "stud ring", he was considerably more apt to put more energy in to running. Mary cackled and was further convinced that she had chosen the right trainer for her four-legged goldmines. Unfortunately, in the state of West Virginia at the time, the first outing for new competitors required they be placed in a "claims" race. If claimed by a bidder, the owner automatically lost the horses to a new owner for the price put on the horse by the owner before the race. If there was more than one bidder, the first one to bid, won the horse. Mary and Mack decided to place a price of three thousand dollars on each horse which was more than they paid for them. That would cover the cost of the trainer, veterinarian, jockey and other expenses. The horses raced and were claimed. At least Mary had satisfied her lifelong dream, made a few dollars on her investment, and found out more "horsey" secrets than she would have ever known. If she had kept the horses, they probably would have become pets as that was her nature.

One day, Catherine was home on holiday, and the four went to the Bowie Race Track. One of the firemen had told Mack to drive around to the back fence instead of going into the business side of the racetrack. They'd find a bookie there, great fried chicken dinners for sale, and maybe a shell game going on as well. That was a memorable day. Some of the local folks had made some terrific fried chicken. Even Cathie enjoyed it. The family watched the shell game for quite a while. Mary gave Catherine a dollar and told her to go and make a bet. Catherine held the dollar ready to play the upcoming game. Cathie was right there about eyeball high to the table. The man displayed the pea, accepted bets, and moved the shells around several times. Cathie was able to follow along at eye level and knew where the pea was located without being noticed. When Catherine was about to make her selection, Cathie prompted her to take the one in the middle. Catherine did and won Five dollars. Cathie then exclaimed, "I saw him move it there". The man quickly told Catherine she was cheating and to move on.

CHAPTER 10

In 1945, Vernon returned home from the war. The war was ending but times were tough and items remained rationed. Vernon returned to his job at Capitol Transit Company. He was soon promoted from bus driver to Depot Clerk, an office job. Catherine, Vernon, and Cathie moved to a small apartment in Clarendon, Virginia. Cathie started first grade at St. Charles Elementary School. There were so many students that year, the class was divided into a morning session and an afternoon session.

It was then Cathie would make a life long friend, Patricia Helen McCausland Maine. During the first month of school, the two girls walked to and from school together. During that time, Cathie would knock on the McCausland front door about seven a.m. so that the girls could attend morning Mass before school. Pat's mother, Geraldine, would open the door to the almost musical sound of Cathie, "Good morning, Mrs. McCausland." Geraldine was not a morning person and the mother of a growing family, Mrs. McCauland's twins, Lee and Eileen were waking about this time as well. Geraldine returned Cathie's greeting most mornings with an "Oh shut up". When the girls would get to Mass, Pat quickly found a place to sit as far away from Cathie as she could. She knew what was coming. The church smelled like incense. The heavy smell frequently caused Cathie to lose her breakfast. It became such a problem that Cathie was excused from having to attend the service. Mary could breathe a sigh of relief not having to deal with Cathie each day but not so for a brand new Nun at St. Charles Elementary School. She would have to face her. The Nun had sent home a note explaining Cathie's refusal to follow instructions when coloring. If the Nun told Cathie to color a bird blue, Cathie would choose to color it purple. A note was sent home requesting her parents to assist with teaching her basic colors. Catherine called Mary for advice but Mary could only offer that Cathie was a very stubborn child. Vernon had a hunch. He was color blind and sure enough, Cathie failed to pass the Chinese Color Test used to identify the problem and she was pronounced color blind as well. For once, she was not just being stubborn and Mary was relieved.

During Cathie's seventh year another big change took place in her life. Mary's brother, Charlie, lost his wife to cancer leaving him with an eleven year old girl, Wendy to care for alone. Mary's solution was for Catherine, Vernon, and Cathie to move in providing extra help for Charlie and a chance for Catherine and Vernon to save money for a home of their own.. Charlie's home was certainly big enough and an agreement was made to do that.

    Cathie loved Uncle Charlie. She tried to love her cousin, Wendy, but it wasn't easy. Wendy did not want another lady in the house and refused to do anything Catherine asked her to do. She was four years older than Cathie and had no interest in anything Cathie liked to do and picked at her every chance she got. Cathie continued to attend Catholic School. Uncle Charlie provided the transportation in his cab from the Maryland suburbs to downtown Washington to small school run by the Sisters of Charity in a poor neighborhood. It was the only Catholic school with an opening at the right price. On the way to school each morning, Uncle Charlie would stop at a small delicatessen, and give Cathie ten cents. With one nickel she was told to play three numbers for him, and with the other nickel she could purchase something for herself. Her purchase was always a Kosher pickle from the barrel.

    When she arrived at school, she smelled like the pickle she enjoyed during the ride. The Nun who greeted her and the other nuns teaching there gave most of their food to the families in the neighborhood leaving very little for themselves. The smell of that pickle was almost too much for the nun. Even though Cathie could not see from the back of the room, she was told to go there each morning because she simply smelled terrible to the starving nun. Within a month of the last day of school, Cathie's nun passed out in class from malnutrition, the school was closed and Cathie began to walk to public school which Cathie preferred.

Each year the family would gather at Charlie's home for Christmas dinner. One Christmas Mary and Mack brought the turkey, Sue and second husband, Curley brought an applesauce cake, Lucy and Earl brought candied sweet potatoes and Catherine provided the rest of the meal. The family was sharing some wine and everyone was in the Christmas sprit until Sue let out a scream and declared someone had pinched her on the fanny. Whether it really happened was never known. Mary assumed Mack was guilty since he was standing next to Sue when Mary saw the two of them and so the blame was placed on him. Mary could never handle wine or any alcoholic beverage. Her reaction to it was red faced, fist in the air, anger. Her temper instantly flared and Mack and Sue were in trouble. Mary instructed Catherine to call a cab. Shortly the cab arrived and Mary snatched the turkey from the oven and headed for the cab. It was approximately thirty miles to Mary's home on the other side of the city.

She was gone and so was turkey. Dinner was memorable for all the wrong reasons. In a few days all the family had made apologies to one another and life went on. That year the Parkers moved to their own home.

Over the years the playhouse became a garden shed as

Cathie had outgrown playing in it. The willow trees had become too large and were dangers to the homes surrounding them. They were removed and Cathie had mixed emotions when seeing the yard without them.

Cathie would visit with Mary and Mack on weekends and during summer vacations. She always enjoyed watching Mary cook and to Mary's delight, the child had finally gotten an appetite. Mary and Cathie would spend hours on the back porch and Mary would tell her about growing up in West Virginia and her early days in Washington. They'd plant a garden and put up watermelon pickles. Over the years, Mary pulled all her own teeth. On occasion, Cathie watched the varied ways Mary went about it. Sometimes Mary would attach a string to the tooth, the other end to a doorknob, and slam the door. Other times she'd use pliers to do the job. Of course, no dentist was able to fit her with false teeth after she had removed every last one of them and for years Mary just did without them. She had a pair of false teeth she'd wear for special occasions, but they ended up in her apron pocket or purse by the end of the day.

When Cathie graduated from high school, visits were less frequent as Cathie was now a secretary for the District of Columbia Schools. Cathie and Mary visited by telephone several times a week and they remained as close as ever. Cathie fell in love with a Navy boy from Pittsburgh when she was twenty. Vernon was not pleased when his only daughter and fishing buddy announced her wedding engagement.

Mary was also not pleased and felt that Cathie needed to date more young men. She hoped she'd find one as she had wanted for Catherine, with money or have potential for that in his future. Mary was even more convinced that Cathie should do more dating after meeting the groom's family. She had invited the groom to be, his parents and Catherine and Vernon over for dinner while the family was visiting from Pittsburgh. Mary had prepared a terrific supper and while it was cooking had served cocktails to her guests on the back porch. The father of the groom was standing at one end of the porch with drink in hand and suddenly fell forward and through the screen, landing in Mary's beautiful bed of Bleeding Hearts. He lay face down. Everyone rushed outside. Big Bill, as he was called, had passed out. He said it was a blood sugar problem but Mary was certain he was a "drinker" and could not hold his liquor. There was no way to convince her that wasn't true and the pleasant afternoon turned sour. Everyone pitched in to make temporary repairs to the porch. Dinner was swift, and the guests made more apologies and quickly left. Mary never got over the incident and was convinced the family was just not right for her granddaughter. Cathie was still headstrong and had made it clear the wedding would be in three months. Mary thought about it and decided to offer her home for the wedding reception even at the risk of additional damage to her porch and offered to pay for it as well.

Cathie thanked her Ganna but said she had paid for her dress and made arrangements for the reception to be held directly behind the church at the local military installation which was free for use to men in service. Mary was furious and refused to attend. She and Mack parked across the street from the church before the ceremony so as to see the bride and groom but not be a part of the affair.

After the honeymoon, Cathie phoned her Grandma to apologize for hurting her feelings and wanted her to know how much she loved and appreciated her. Mary hung up on Cathie and after much thought, called to tell Cathie she'd thought about what a hard headed child she had always been and she'd just have to live with it the way she'd always done. The two kept in touch and enjoyed their continued visits and phone calls.

Three years passed and one day Cathie called with great news. She was pregnant and Mary was overjoyed at the thought of being a great-grandmother. When Cathie gave birth to a son, Anthony Steven, Mary was quick to denounce the name he'd been given declaring that she'd be calling him Steven as that was Irish. The Italian name was not to her liking. All things Italian were not offensive to Mary as she loved Cathie's Lasagna and wanted the recipe for the "La zon za".

As time went by, Cathie and family, moved to Norfolk, Virginia. Mary and Mack went to visit and enjoyed playing with little Tony. Mary and Catherine often spent time reminiscing about Cathie and all the problems she'd brought to them. They could laugh about them now that time had passed and the bad memories had time to fade a bit. Mary would recall Cathie's swollen feet and the many times she'd disobeyed her going barefoot in the yard. She'd walk through the clover; a bee would sting her, and she'd spend the next day or two on the back porch soaking her foot or plastering it with baking soda. She never seemed to learn to put on those shoes in the summer. Mary would cringe each time she'd remember the times when she'd have to administer milk of magnesia or an enema to that screaming, squirming little bit of a girl. She'd think about how many meals she'd "doctored" with ketchup, mustard, and even Worcestershire sauce to get the child to eat. She'd smile when she recalled how her brother, Dave, put mustard in the diaper of a doll Cathie got for Christmas and the look on Cathie's tearful face when she discovered it. She remembered how Cathie would run to her mother when the Air Raid sirens would sound during World War II there in the suburbs of Washington, D. C. as the city would practice for attacks that fortunately never happened. Mack would bring home clothes collected at the engine house for war orphans that were the size Mary had told him to find. Cathie would try them on and get to keep the ones that fit. Her outgrown clothes were sent back to the engine house to replace the ones brought home. Mary also remembered the time Cathie saved her from a terrible fate. Mary had gotten a new wringer washing machine when Cathie was visiting one weekend. The first day she was to try it, she and Cathie took the clothes to the basement, filled the wringer-washer, and washed the clothes. Mary had never used the wringer before. She took the laundered clothes and decided to put them through the ringer before rinsing them. As Mary put a shirt through the wringer, her apron string became folded in the shirt. During the process her apron and dress were being drawn uncomfortably tight and Mary began to gasp for breath. Mary screamed, "Cathie, hit it, hit it." Cathie didn't know what to hit, but as luck would have it, landed a blow on the wringer release bar, disengaging it and the machinery stopped dead. Dump had finally been of help.

Cathie had a lifetime of memories of Mary as well. She remembered their trip across town on a streetcar when she was about four. They were going to meet Mack and go to the races. He had been working at a different engine house and they would meet at the platform on Pennsylvania Avenue near the Sousa Bridge and go on to the races in Bowie, Maryland. When Cathie and Mary stepped off the streetcar and sat down to wait for Mack, a man came along pulling a Billy goat on a rope. He'd stopped to talk to another man and the goat was grazing along side the road in the grass.

Cathie could not resist any animal and was soon petting the goat. The goat was in no mood to be disturbed and turned quickly to "butt" Cathie. Mary jumped up and started beating the animal with her purse and when the man tried to stop her, she started beating him. Things quickly got out of hand and a policeman threatened Mary with arrest and told the man to remove the goat.

She recalled a trip shopping with Mary and baby, Tony. Mary wanted to buy an outfit for the child. When they found one, Mary looked in her purse and found there was not quite enough money in her billfold. The store was quite crowded but Mary was determined to make her purchase. She stuck her right hand down the front of her dress and began feeling for something down there. People began to notice Mary's antics as Cathie held Mary's purse in one hand and her baby in the other arm.

Mary yelled. "IT'S GONE!" She continued to search for something and yelling over and over, "IT'S GONE!" Finally, she smiled and withdrew a little white bag, tied with string. It was her stash of cash she kept tucked under her breast, deep in her enormous bra. With that, the crowd dispersed and the shopping trip was done. God bless Mary.

Mary and Mack spent their retirement years between home on Leland Street in the summer and a motel in Hialeah, Florida near the racetrack in the winter. Mary loved the change of seasons spending time with the family in summer and with her precious horses and racing friends in Florida in the winter. Life had become fun year round.

When Mary was seventy-six she suffered a stroke. She

lost some use of her left arm, walked with the help of a cane, and her speech was slightly affected. The year that followed was a tough one for both Mary and Mack. They did spend the winter in Hialeah just the same, but in the spring Mary lost her will to live and soon went on to be with the angels.

Mary had accumulated quite a large amount of money thanks to all those years renting rooms and saving faithfully and Mack quickly enjoyed a high time in Hialeah. He had been more than rewarded for being the wonderful husband she had hoped to find.

Catherine, Cathie and the family wept and shared their stories about Mary. LIFE WAS GOOD and memories of her could fill a book.

CPSIA information can be obtained at www.ICGtesting.com
Printed in the USA
LVOW061040131011
250304LV00003B/7/P